JET FIGHTERS

BY DENNY VON FINN

TORQUE

BELLWETHER MEDIA • MINNEAPOLIS, MN

TM

Are you ready to take it to the extreme? Torque books thrust you into the action-packed world of sports, vehicles, and adventure. These books may include dirt, smoke, fire, and dangerous stunts. WARNING: read at your own risk.

This edition first published in 2010 by Bellwether Media, Inc.

Library of Congress Cataloging-in-Publication Data

Von Finn, Denny.
Jet fighters / by Denny Von Finn.
p. cm. -- (Torque books : the world's fastest)
Includes bibliographical references and index.
Summary: "Amazing photography accompanies engaging information about jet fighters. The combination of high-interest subject matter and light text is intended for students in grades 3 through 7"--Provided by publisher.
ISBN 978-1-60014-335-9 (hardcover : alk. paper)
1. Fighter planes--Juvenile literature. I. Title.
UG1242.F5V66 2010
623.74'64--dc22 2009037749

Printed in the United States of America, North Mankato, MN.

010110 1149

CONTENTS

What Are Jet Fighters?

Jet fighters are **military aircraft**. Some can reach speeds of 1,500 miles (2,400 kilometers) per hour. They are armed with guns, missiles, and bombs. They have high-tech equipment like lasers and **heat sensors**. These tools help pilots carry out dangerous missions at **supersonic** speeds.

Most jet fighters are made for **dogfights**. Jet engines give pilots speed and **maneuverability**. Skilled pilots change direction quickly. This allows them to sneak up on enemy aircraft. Pilots also use speed to surprise enemies on the ground.

Messerschmitt Me 262

Fast Fact

In 2008, the U.S. government hired a company to develop a laser weapon small enough to be carried in a jet fighter.

The first jet fighter was the Messerschmitt Me 262. The Germans used it at the end of World War II. The Me 262 had a great speed advantage over other fighters.

Other militaries started to build jet fighters after World War II. The United States and Russia have made the best fighters since then.

Jet Fighter Technology

A jet fighter has one or more jet engines. A fan pulls air into a jet engine. The air is mixed with burning fuel. It becomes very hot and expands. Then the air rushes out the back of the engine. The rushing air creates **thrust**. The thrust pushes the jet fighter forward.

Fast Fact

Drones are unmanned aircraft. They are controlled with joysticks thousands of miles from battle. Some experts believe drones will replace jet fighters within the next 50 years.

A jet fighter's **airframe** has a sleek shape. This reduces **friction**. Friction slows down aircraft. Friction also makes the airframe very hot in flight. Airframes are made of heat-resistant materials like **titanium** to withstand this heat.

Fast Fact

Some jet fighters use stealth technology. Their paint and the shapes of their airframes help them escape enemy radar.

The pilot sits in the **cockpit**. A **control column** is used to control the aircraft. The pilot must watch several screens in the cockpit. The screens show information about the aircraft. They also warn of enemy aircraft and vehicles.

The Future of Jet Fighters

Militaries need jet fighters that can do many jobs. The T-50 is a Russian fighter in development. It will be able to attack targets on land, in the sea, and in the air. The T-50 will have a **range** of more than 2,500 miles (4,000 kilometers). It will have a top speed of 1,300 miles (2,100 kilometers) per hour.

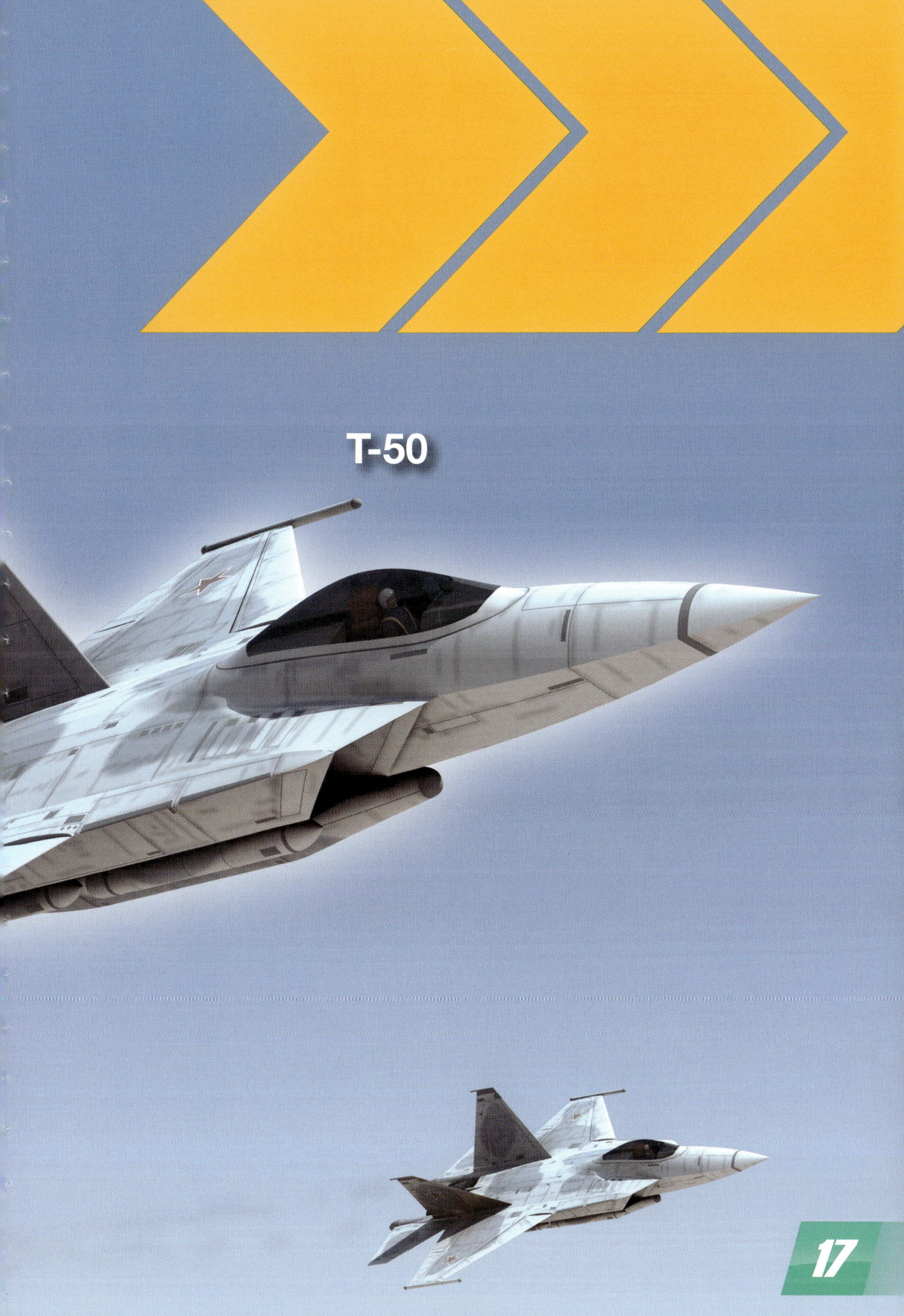
T-50

The F-35 Lightning II is another jet fighter of the future. It will also have a top speed of about 1,300 miles (2,100 kilometers) per hour. Fighters that fly at high speeds use a lot of fuel. Some F-35 fighters will carry more than 20,000 pounds (9,100 kilograms) of fuel.

F-35 Lightning II

Fast Fact

Some scientists believe that future hypersonic jets will be able to travel at Mach 15!

The F-35 and T-50 will one day be replaced. Future jet fighters might be **hypersonic**. Today's militaries are testing unmanned jets. Future jet pilots could one day carry out their missions far from the battle. The Boeing X-43 is one such jet. In 2004, it reached nearly 7,000 miles (11,265 kilometers) per hour!

GLOSSARY

airframe—the body and wings of an aircraft

cockpit—the area in a jet fighter where the pilot sits

control column—the stick a pilot uses to control a jet fighter

dogfights—one-on-one combat between jet fighters in the sky

friction—a force created when two objects rub against each other

heat sensors—devices on jet fighters that detect the heat given off by enemy aircraft, trucks, tanks, and buildings

hypersonic—describes an aircraft that travels around 3,500 miles (5,600 kilometers) per hour or more

maneuverability—the ability to make quick, precise turns, especially at high speeds

military aircraft—airplanes designed for use in combat

range—the distance a jet fighter can travel before running out of fuel

supersonic—faster than the speed of sound, which is 761 miles (1,225 kilometers) per hour at sea level with a temperature of 59° F (15° C)

thrust—a force created by jet engines that pushes a jet fighter forward

titanium—a lightweight, heat-resistant metal used to build jet fighters

TO LEARN MORE

AT THE LIBRARY

Alvarez, Carlos. *F/A-18E/F Super Hornets*. Minneapolis, Minn.: Bellwether Media, 2010.

Von Finn, Denny. *Supersonic Jets*. Minneapolis, Minn.: Bellwether Media, 2010.

Zobel, Derek. *F-22 Raptors*. Minneapolis, Minn.: Bellwether Media, 2009.

ON THE WEB

Learning more about jet fighters is as easy as 1, 2, 3.

1. Go to www.factsurfer.com.
2. Enter "jet fighters" into the search box.
3. Click the "Surf" button and you will see a list of related Web sites.

With factsurfer.com, finding more information is just a click away.

INDEX

The images in this book are reproduced through the courtesy of: Stocktrek/Getty images, front cover, p. 6; United States Department of Defense, pp. 4-5, 7, 8, 9, 10-11, 12-13, 14, 15, 18-19, 20-21; Jozef Gatial, pp. 16-17.